Burglars, Ducks and Kissing Frogs
HUMOROUS SHORT STORIES

Contents

Burglars 3
by Norman Hunter
illustrated by Lynne Chapman

Duck Boy 15
by Jeremy Strong
illustrated by Nick Diggory

Kissy, Kissy 31
by Louise Cooper
illustrated by Simon Jacob

Duck Boy © Jeremy Strong 2003
Kissy, Kissy © Louise Cooper 2003
Series editors: Martin Coles and Christine Hall

PEARSON EDUCATION LIMITED
Edinburgh Gate
Harlow
Essex CM20 2JE
England

www.longman.co.uk

The right of Norman Hunter, Jeremy Strong and Louise Cooper to be identified as the authors of this work has been asserted by them in accordance with the Copyright, Designs and Patents Act, 1988.

We are grateful to The Random House Group Limited for permission to reproduce an extract from *The Incredible Adventures of Professor Branestawm* by Norman Hunter published by Bodley Head.

All rights reserved. No part of this publication may be reproduced, stored in a retrieval system, or transmitted in any form or by any means, electronic, mechanical, photocopying, recording, or otherwise without either the prior written permission of the Publishers or a licence permitting restricted copying in the United Kingdom issued by the Copyright Licensing Agency Ltd, 90 Tottenham Court Road, London W1P 9HE.

First published 2003
ISBN 0582 79620 2

Illustrated by Lynne Chapman (PFD), Nick Diggory and
Simon Jacob (Sylvie Poggio)

Printed in Great Britain by Scotprint, Haddington

The publishers' policy is to use paper manufactured from sustainable forests.

Burglars
by Norman Hunter

Professor Branestawm rang the bell for his housekeeper, and then, remembering that he'd taken the bell away to invent a new kind of one, he went out into the kitchen to find her.

"Mrs Flittersnoop," he said, looking at her through his glasses and holding the other four pairs, "put your things on and come to the pictures with me. There is a film on this evening about the home life of the Brussels sprout."

"Thank you kindly, sir," said Mrs Flittersnoop. "I won't take a minute, and I'll be ready." She didn't care about the Brussels sprout picture, but she wanted to see the Mickey Mouse one. So, while the Professor was putting on his boots and taking them off again because he had them on the wrong feet, and getting some money out of his money box with a bit of wire, she put on her best bonnet, and off they went.

* * * * *

"Dear, dear," said the Professor when they got back from the pictures. "I don't remember leaving that window open, but I'm glad we did because I forgot my latchkey."

"Goodness gracious!" cried Mrs Flittersnoop. The room was all anyhow.

"The other rooms are the same," called the Professor from the top of the stairs. "Burglars have been."

And so they had. While the Professor and his housekeeper had been at the pictures thieves had broken in.

They'd stolen the Professor's silver teapot that his auntie gave him, and the butter dish he was going to give his auntie, only he forgot. They'd taken the Professor's best eggcups that were never used, except on Sundays.

"This is all wrong," said the Professor, coming downstairs and running in and out of the rooms and keeping on finding more things that had gone. "I won't have it. I'm going to invent a burglar catcher; that's what I'm going to invent."

"We'd better get a policeman first," said Mrs Flittersnoop. So the Professor fetched a policeman, who brought another policeman, and they both went into the kitchen and had a cup of tea, while the Professor went into his inventory to invent his burglar catcher and Mrs Flittersnoop went to bed.

Next morning the Professor was still inventing. It was lucky the burglars hadn't stolen his inventory, but they couldn't do that because it was too heavy to take away. They couldn't even take any of the Professor's inventing tools, because the door had a special Professor lock that didn't open with a key at all but only when you squeezed some toothpaste into it and then blew through the keyhole. And, of course, the burglars didn't know about that. They never do know about things of that sort.

"How far have you got with the burglar catcher?" asked Mrs Flittersnoop presently, coming in with breakfast.

"Not very far yet," he said. In fact, he'd only got as far as nailing two pieces of wood together and starting to think what to do next. So he stopped for a bit and had his breakfast.

Then he went on inventing day and night for ever so long.

"Come and see the burglar catcher," he said one day.

"Bless me!" said Mrs Flittersnoop. "It looks like a mangle with a lot of arms."

"Now watch," said the Professor. He brought out a bolster with his overcoat tied round it and they went round outside the window.

"This is a dummy burglar," he explained. "In he goes." He opened the window and pushed the dummy inside.

Immediately there were a lot of clicking and whirring noises. Wheels began to go round and things began to squeak and whizz. And the window closed itself behind the dummy.

"It's working, it's working," cried the Professor, dancing with joy.

Suddenly the clicking and whizzing stopped, a trapdoor opened in the study floor and something fell through it. Then a bell rang.

bolster: a large long pillow

"That's the alarm," said the Professor, rushing away. "It means the burglar thing's caught a burglar."

He led the way down into the cellar, and there on the cellar floor was the bolster with the overcoat on. And it was all tied up with ropes so that it looked like one of those mummy things out of a museum. You could hardly see any bolster or coat at all, it was so tied up.

"Well I never," said Mrs Flittersnoop.

The Professor undid the bolster and put his overcoat on. Then he went upstairs and wound the burglar catcher up again, put on Mrs Flittersnoop's bonnet by mistake and went to the pictures again. He wanted to see the Brussels sprout film once more, because he'd missed bits of it before through Mrs Flittersnoop keeping on talking to him about her sister Aggie.

Mrs Flittersnoop had finished all her housework by the time the pictures were over. But the Professor didn't come in. Quite a long time afterwards he didn't come in. She wondered where he could have got to.

"Forgotten where he lives, I expect," she said. "I'd better get a policeman to look for him."

But just as she was going to do that, 'br-r-r-ring-ing-ing-g-g' went the Professor's burglar catcher.

"There now," cried Mrs Flittersnoop. "A burglar and all. And just when the Professor isn't here to see his machine thing catch him. Tut, tut."

She picked up the rolling pin and ran down into the cellar. Yes, it was a burglar all right. There he lay on the cellar floor all tied up with rope so he looked like a mummy out of a museum. And like the bolster dummy, he was so tied up you could hardly see any of him.

"Ha," cried the housekeeper, "I'll teach you to burgle, that I will," but she didn't teach him that at all. She hit him on the head with the rolling pin, just to make quite sure he shouldn't get away. Then she ran out and got the policeman she was going to fetch to look for the Professor.

And the policeman took the burglar away in a wheelbarrow to the police station, all tied up and hit on the head as he was. And the burglar went very quietly. He couldn't do anything else.

But the Professor didn't come home. The police didn't find him. They hunted everywhere. They looked under the seat at the pictures, but all they found was Mrs Flittersnoop's bonnet, which they took to the police station as evidence, if you know what that is. Anyhow, they took it whether you know or not.

"Where can he be?" said the housekeeper. "Oh! He is a careless man to go losing himself like that!"

Then, when they'd hunted a lot more and still hadn't found the Professor, the Judge said it was time to try the new burglar they'd caught. So they put him in the prisoner's place in the court.

"You are charged with being a burglar inside Professor Branestawm's house," said the Judge. "What do you mean by it?"

But the prisoner couldn't speak. He was too tied up to do more than wriggle.

"Ha," said the Judge, "nothing to say for yourself, and I should think not, too."

Then the policeman undid the ropes and things. And there was such a lot of them that they filled the court up, and everyone was struggling about in long snaky sort of tapes and ropes and it was ever so long before they could get all sorted out again.

"Goodness gracious me!" cried Mrs Flittersnoop. "If it isn't the Professor!"

It was the Professor. There he was in the prisoner's place.

"What's all this?" said the Judge.

"Please, I'm Professor Branestawm," said the Professor, taking off all his five pairs of glasses, and bowing to the court.

"Well," snapped the Judge. He was very cross. "What has that got to do with anything? Didn't you break into the Professor's house?"

"I left my key at home and got in through the window," said the Professor, "forgetting about the burglar catcher."

"That is neither here nor there," said the Judge, "You broke into the Professor's house. You can't deny it."

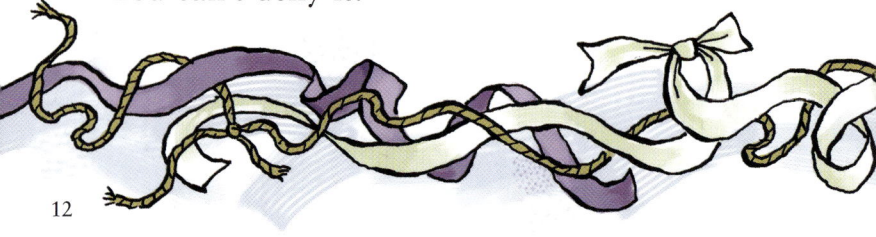

"But it was my own house," said the Professor.

"All the more reason why you shouldn't break into it," said the Judge. "What's the front door for?"

"I forgot the key," said the Professor.

"Don't argue," said the Judge, and he held up Mrs Flittersnoop's bonnet that the Professor had worn by mistake and left under the seat at the pictures. "This bonnet, I understand, belongs to your housekeeper."

Mrs Flittersnoop got up and bowed. "Indeed it does, your Majesty," she said, thinking that was the right way to speak to a judge, "but the Professor's welcome to it, I'm sure, if he wants it."

"There you are," said the Judge, "she says 'he's welcome to it if he wants it'. That means she didn't give it to him, did you?"

"No," said Mrs Flittersnoop, "I thought …"

"What you thought isn't evidence," snapped the Judge.

"Well, what is evidence, then?" said Mrs Flittersnoop, beginning to get cross. "I never heard of the stuff. And I'm tired of all this talk that I don't understand. Give me my best bonnet and let me go. I've the dinner to get."

"Oh, give the woman her bonnet," said the Judge, and then he turned to the Professor. "If it had been anybody else's house you'd broken into," he said, "we'd have put you in prison."

"Of course," said the Professor.

"But," thundered the Judge, getting all worked up, "as it was you who broke into the house and as it was your own house you broke into, we can only sentence you to be set free, and a fine waste of good time this trial has been."

At this everyone in the court cheered, for most of them knew the Professor and liked him and were glad everything was going to be all right.

And as for Mrs Flittersnoop, she clapped her bonnet on the Professor's head, and then several people carried him shoulder-high out of the court and home, with the Professor bowing and smiling and looking through first one pair of glasses and then another.

Duck Boy
by Jeremy Strong

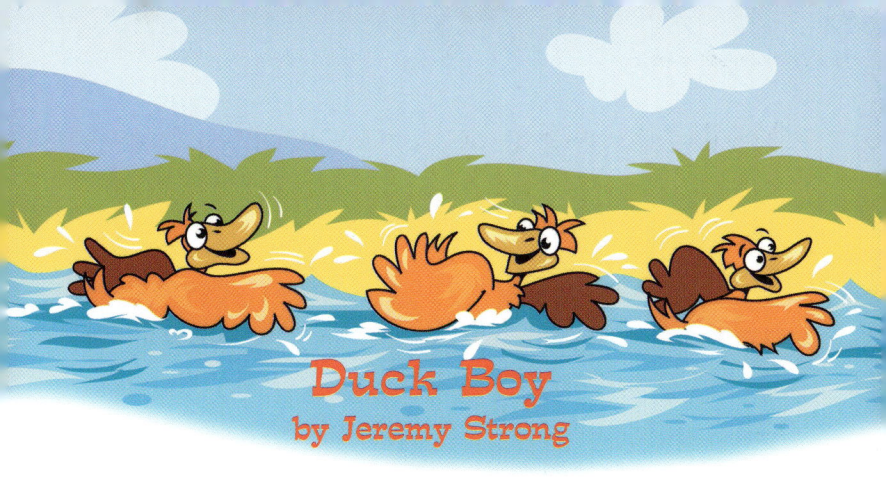

This story begins with a tragedy but ends happily. There! Now I've spoiled everything and told you the ending before I've properly begun. Then again, maybe I haven't, because it is really what happens in the middle that makes this story so strange.

A mother was taking her baby son for a walk. Her son James was just three months old. She put James in his little pram and pushed him along the pathway beside the river.

The path followed the river right out into the countryside. The mother did not often go as far as that. There was a bench where she always stopped. She would sit down and have a little rest before starting back home. The bench was on the top of a little hill, overlooking the river and the countryside. It was a good place to stop.

One day the mother stopped at the bench as usual and she parked the pram next to her. Maybe it was because the sun felt so soft and warm on her face. Maybe it was the sound of the birds singing. Maybe it was because James was teething and his new teeth hurt and that had made him cry half the night and kept both of them awake.

Anyhow, the mother fell asleep.

James, however, did not fall asleep. He threw his rattle out of the pram. He threw his blanket out of the pram. He chucked out teddy and rabbit.

Now, just as James was chucking stuff out of his pram, a very untidy old lady was chucking stuff out of her kitchen.

She had just bought herself a new, red washing-up bowl. She flung the old one out of the window. It landed in the river and away it bobbed.

By this time James had nothing left to throw out so he made some very sloppy noises and filled his nappy. He was bored. Very bored.

All this time his mother slept on. The washing-up bowl bobbed nearer and nearer to where the pram stood.

James grabbed the sides of his pram and he began to shake it. He bounced up and down. He rocked from side to side. The pram rolled forward a little way. James rocked and shook and bounced. The pram moved forward a little faster as it reached the slope of the little hill. And then, whoosh! Off went the pram, whizzing down the hill, while James laughed and gurgled and rocked and bounced.

And the washing-up bowl danced closer and closer.

Back on the bench his mother started to snore.

The pram finally reached the riverbank and hit a fallen branch at full speed. The pram went head over tail into the fast waters of the river. As for James, he was hurled from the pram, high into the air. Round and round he spun, right out over the river. Then down he came, down, down, down until ...

whump!

He landed in the washing-up bowl, which had reached that part of the river just at the right moment. What a stroke of luck!

The bowl, with James inside,

went off down the river, gently bobbing up and down. He dabbled his fingers in the water and laughed when the little fish tickled his fingers. He gazed at the ducks and geese and swans. At last he fell asleep.

Back on the bench, the mother woke up. Oh horror! She was tearing out her hair and wailing away. "Where's my son?" Then she saw the pram in the river. It was empty. The mother could hardly bear to breathe any longer. Her son was dead, and it was all her fault.

Of course, you and I know it wasn't all her

fault because James had done a lot of bouncing and rocking and so on. But the mother was heartbroken.

The washing-up bowl carried him a long way from the town. He went on down the river until nightfall, when the bowl caught in some tree branches over the river, and it stayed there until morning, when James woke up and began to cry. He was hungry. His teeth hurt. His nappy needed changing.

* * * * *

A family of ducks heard James crying.
"A baby human!" said Father Duck.
"All on its own!" said Mother Duck. "We had better look after it."

They grabbed the washing-up bowl with their beaks and they pulled it across to their nest. They pushed and shoved until they got that bowl out of the water and into the nest. The five ducklings in the nest were not pleased to be sharing their bed with a washing-up bowl full of three-month-old baby and a stinky nappy.

But the parents said the baby needed their help. "When a human finds a duckling all on its own they pick it up and look after it, so we are doing the same thing, but the other way round. This baby needs a home and parents and brothers and sisters just as you do. We shall all help look after it."

That is exactly what they did. James was well cared for in the ducks' nest. They fed him with waterweed and little snails and all things green and gloopy. They changed his nappy and washed him in the river. They told him bedtime stories about the great duck heroes of the past – Donald, Jemima and Daffy. In fact, they treated him just like their own little ducklings.

The days he spent with the duck family turned into weeks. The weeks became months and then years.

James learned everything from the ducks. His first word was 'Quack!' In fact his second word was 'Quack!' too, and so were the third and fourth, but at least the ducks knew what he was talking about.

They taught him how to swim, and in fact James paddled before he could walk. He became very good at swimming. The duck family taught James duck-paddle of course, but James could do something else that was quite new to the ducks. He could do front crawl with his arms, and by combining this with duck-paddle he was much faster than the ducks.

"That is brilliant!" cried Father Duck. "How do you do that?"

So James taught the duck family how to do

front crawl. The ducks found it very difficult at first because they were not used to making one wing do something different from the other wing.

They went round in circles, splashing everyone and everything. But bit by bit the ducks learned how to do front crawl with their wings, and then they became the fastest ducks on the river. In fact, they were the fastest ducks ever.

James taught them backstroke too, and the duck family could often be seen out with James, lazily swimming on their backs and sunning their bellies.

Ducks from miles around would come and watch in astonishment. They wanted to know how it was done. James began teaching front crawl to all the water birds and soon the sky was filled with birds arriving to join his swimming classes. One clever bird soon realised that if she could swim faster by doing front crawl then perhaps it would help her fly faster, too. She tried it out and it did. She could fly three times faster than before! On her back, too!

It was not long before the skies were full of birds rocketing past at hyper-speed. As for the river – it was as if all the ducks had turned into mini powerboats.

Obviously it would not be long before people began to notice.

A large party of hunters came to the river one

evening to do some duck shooting. They were astonished to see so many ducks everywhere – great flapping piles of them! The ducks were so busy looping the loop and stunt flying, they didn't even notice the hunters.

The hunters began banging away with their guns. What a surprise they got! Those birds were faster than bullets! They went whooshing right past the hunters. They went whizzing up into the sky like rockets. They were so fast the hunters got dizzy and fell over in a heap in the water. They trudged off home, soaking wet, without a single dead duck.

The ducks were very happy with the way things had turned out. They felt that James had saved their lives. But James pointed out that if the ducks had not looked after him when he arrived in the washing-up bowl he would not be alive himself.

All in all everyone was very happy – all except for James' mother. Three years had now passed since James had gone, but she had never got over that terrible day. She had shut herself indoors ever since and spent most of the day staring at the television.

Sometimes she switched it on.

The hunters could not stop talking to each other about how those ducks had escaped.

"Did you see how fast they could fly? It was almost as if they were swimming through the sky!"

"I saw one doing backstroke!"

"And one looked like a baby boy. Strange. Very strange."

The hunters told their friends. The friends told their friends. More and more people heard about the speeding ducks. More and more people went down to the river to watch them. In the midst of all this was James. He still couldn't fly – he had tried many times, but he just could not do it. But he joined in all the river stuff – all that turbo paddling and so on.

The newspapers and TV shows got to hear about it. One day James woke up to find the bank of the river completely covered with camera crews and reporters. The main news that night was full of the story of the amazing ducks and Duck Boy. (In other words, James.)

"It's true," said the newscaster. "It is just like the story of Tarzan, the boy who was brought up by apes. But this little baby was raised by a family of ducks. The local hunters call him Duck Boy."

It just so happened that on this day James' real mother had decided to switch on her television. Her mouth fell open. Could it be? Could it?

The boy looked just like James. He was bigger of course, but he had the same blue eyes, the same smile. Her heart began to beat faster and faster. She could hardly bear it. She ran down to the river. Her heart was thundering and her brain was asking the same question over and over again. Is it really James?

When she reached the river she pushed through the crowd, her heart full of hope.

And then she saw James. He was older and bigger and dirtier but it was James. She knew at once. Before she even knew what she was doing she started to make her way towards him. She held out her arms to her son and called.

"James! James! It's me – your mother!"
James splashed and stopped swimming. There was something familiar about the voice that called him. He watched the woman coming towards him.

"James! It's me!"

"Quack?" said James, because of course he could only speak Duck.

James' mother stopped dead. Quack? Was that the way to greet your long lost mother? For a moment she was angry and then she realised, that of course James would speak Duck. So she answered him like this: "Quack!"

"Quack!" cried James.

"Quack, quack!" shouted James's mother, pushing towards him even faster.

"Quack, QUACK! QUACK!" yelled James. They understood each other perfectly!

So it all ended happily after all. What a story! There was only one thing left to decide. Would James go back to land and live with his real mum, or would his real mum get into the river, learn to swim and be a duck? What do you think?

I can tell you that James himself became the greatest Olympic swimmer on Earth, even though he had a rather odd style. He cannot swim without quacking an awful lot, and very loudly. Olympic swimming events were very noisy for many years.

* * * * *

The moral of this story is: be kind to ducks; you never know when you might need their help.

Kissy, Kissy
by Louise Cooper

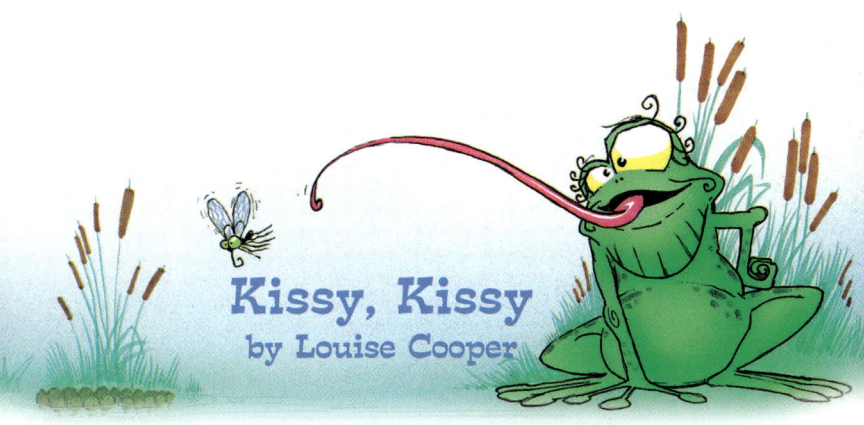

Gogglina the frog had lived in the palace pond since she was a tadpole. She reckoned it was pretty okay. There were lily pads to jump on, and loads of flies and slugs and other lovely things to eat. And Grandma Glugga, who ruled the pond, said it had the best mud in the whole kingdom.

Grandma Glugga spent most of her time in the mud. She didn't know half of what Gogglina and her friends got up to. She didn't see them when they sprang out of the pond to scare passing Princesses. She didn't notice when, at the evening croak-ins, they sang rude words to all the old songs.

And she didn't notice the Prince.

Gogglina did, though. He didn't do the things

princes normally did, like play football or gallop around on a horse shouting 'Yo!' Instead, he sat near the pond, *sighing*. Gogglina was puzzled. Princesses sighed a lot, but they were soppy. Princes should be different. This prince was gloomy, too. Something was obviously wrong.

Frogs weren't supposed to talk to humans. In fact, humans weren't supposed to know that frogs *could* talk. But one morning, as the Prince sat sighing as usual, Gogglina hopped onto a lily leaf and said,

"Hello! Why are you such a misery guts?"

She expected the Prince to yell in surprise. But instead he cried happily, "You recognise me!"

"*Eh?*" croaked Gogglina. "Recognise you? 'Course I don't! What are you on about?"

"I'm not a prince!" cried the Prince. "I'm a frog, just like you!"

"*Eh?*" said Gogglina again.

"I was turned into a prince by a horrible, wicked witch," he told her. "It was really unfair; I mean, I didn't *know* it was her pet wasp when I ate it! But she put a spell on me, and now I'm … *human!*" He shuddered.

"Wow!" said Gogglina. "How *revolting!* Poor you!"

"That's why I'm so miserable," said the Prince – or frog. "There's only one way to undo the spell, you see. I've got to be kissed by a girl frog." He gazed at her. "*You're* the most beautiful girl frog I've ever seen."

"Am I?" said Gogglina, going all wriggly inside. "Really?"

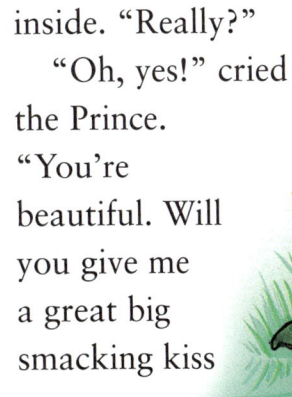

"Oh, yes!" cried the Prince. "You're beautiful. Will you give me a great big smacking kiss and turn me into myself again? Oh, please!"

Gogglina didn't know what to do. Okay, she was sorry for the Prince – or frog. Who wouldn't be? But the idea of *kissing* him … that was truly *gross!* All that horrible pink skin, without a trace of proper green; and that creepy-crawly hair stuff on his head … And the things that humans ate: *cake* and *peanut butter* and *ice cream* … *Yuk!* It made her feel sick just to think about it!

"Please!" begged the Prince again. He puckered his mouth and shut his eyes. "Just one! That's all it needs. And you're *so* beautiful …"

Gogglina did feel sorry for him; she really did. But –

"No *way!*" she croaked in horror. And she dived to the bottom of the pond to find Grandma Glugga.

* * * * *

"Wicked witch, pooey!" Grandma Glugga snorted. "I don't believe a word of it. If you ask me, that story is a load of old snail slime. He's a nasty human, and he's trying to fool you. Of *course* he wants a kiss from a girl frog. They all do, you know. Think what it must be like to have to kiss a crawly, pink princess – *urrgh!* If he says he's a frog, he's got to prove it."

"How, Grandma?" said Gogglina.

"By doing the things all frogs *can* do, of course. For instance, how far can he jump?"

"I didn't ask," said Gogglina.

"More fool you, then. How many flies can he catch in one minute? If he can't catch flies, then he's no better than he should be and ought to do somersaults." (Grandma Glugga had lots of favourite sayings, and most of them didn't make much sense.) "Can he croak the latest songs? Can he croak *at all?*"

"I don't know," said Gogglina, feeling silly.

"Well then," said Grandma "I'll have a word with this prince. Because no grand-tadpole of mine's going to make herself ill by kissing a *human* unless there's a good reason."

* * * * *

The Prince was blubbing by the side of the pond when Gogglina and Grandma Glugga popped their heads above the water. Grandma snorted, "Cry-baby! He ought to have his nobbles gurgled!" But when he saw them he cheered up.

"I can prove I'm a frog!" he said. "I never boast, but in my proper shape I could jump across this pond from one side to the other! And I could eat *squillions* of flies a minute. And croak any hit song!"

"Hmmph!" said Grandma Glugga. "You never boast, eh? Well, you're going to have to prove it. And in human shape, too."

The Prince's face fell. "Don't I get the kiss first?" he asked.

"Not while I've still got blobs on my grummet!" said Grandma. "Come on, my lad – it's test time."

* * * * *

By the time the Prince's test began, every frog in the pond had come to watch.

The Prince – who said that his frog name was Golp – crouched at the edge of the pond. Grandma Glugga was on the far side, and Gogglina was next to her.

"Right!" shouted Grandma. "First test – lily pad jumping. On your marks!"

The Prince puffed his chest out.

"Get set!" yelled Grandma.

The Prince stuck his elbows out.

"GO!" bellowed Grandma.

And this is what they heard:

"Yeee-HAAA!" That was the Prince.

Sproing! That was the Prince jumping.

Wheee ... That was the noise of him flying through the air.

WALLOP! That was the sound of him landing on the lily pad. So far, so good.

Then:

Splob. That was the lily pad tipping over under the Prince's weight. The Prince said something like, "Ooh-er ... yipes ... WAAAH ..."

And the next noises went like this:

"*Aaarrgh!*"

Ker-SPLOSH!

"*Guggle ... globble ... urrrk ... glug-glug-glug ...*"

SKWUDGE.

For a few moments there was complete silence. Then the croaking began, as the frogs laughed themselves sick.

A passing princess screamed and ran away, but the frogs took no notice. They clutched each other, rolling on their backs and kicking their legs in the air. The Prince was spitting out black blobs of mud as he struggled up. He looked like a black blob himself. The frogs hooted more than ever, until Grandma Glugga's voice bellowed, "That's enough!"

"PTOO!" The Prince spat out more mud. "How did I do?" he asked sadly.

"Middling," said Grandma. "Come on, come on! Time for your next test."

"Er … which one's that?" asked the Prince nervously.

Grandma grinned across her whole face, in the way that only frogs can.

"Flies," she said.

* * * * *

Bzzzz …
SNAP!

Zee-owww! The fly zipped away, and the Prince sat rubbing his jaw. "Ow," he said. "That *hurt.*"

"Any *real* frog knows you use your tongue!" Grandma Glugga eyed a passing gnat, then her own tongue went *flick*. The gnat never knew a thing about it.

"But my tongue isn't long enough!" the Prince wailed. He gazed at Gogglina. "You really *are* beautiful. Can't I have the kiss now? *Please?*"

"Certainly not!" snorted Grandma. "Come on! Your total so far is one housefly, two greenflies, half a bumble-bee and a maybug. I don't call *that* very good!"

"But they make me feel sick," moaned the Prince.

"What?" Grandma was outraged. "I never thought I'd live to hear a frog say such a thing! I think you're *definitely* not a frog at all."

"I am, I am!" the Prince wailed. "It's only because I've got a human body that I don't like eating flies! If I was in my proper shape, I'd *love* them!"

"He is greener than he was, Grandma," said Gogglina. "Look at his face."

"We-ell … I suppose he *is* a bit more frog-coloured," Grandma Glugga admitted. "All right then. Try again. Bluebottles, greenbottles, bees, fleas, anything with wings, anything that stings –"

"I don't want to get stung!" wailed the Prince.

"Oh, stop being a weedy-globber and get on with it!" said Grandma.

* * * * *

The Prince swallowed twenty-three flying insects before he had to run away and be sick. Grandma Glugga admitted that now he really *had* turned a nice shade of green. His eyes were starting to bulge, too.

"Right," she said, when the Prince tottered back. "One last test."

The Prince gazed at Gogglina. "Can't I have –"

"No!" Grandma said. "Song time first. Start with the one that goes: *Rrrrrak-rrak-ribbit, kek, kek, kek!*"

"I know it!" cried the Prince, and started to sing. "*Ooo, baby, ya really got me hoppin'* –"

"Don't sing it!" Grandma was outraged. "Croak it!"

"Oh." The Prince's face fell. "It won't be as good as my frog voice. If I could only have –"

"GET ON WITH IT!" bawled Grandma.

The Prince sighed. "All right." He looked at Gogglina again. "I'll sing it especially for you. It's a *love* song."

Gogglina blushed, which for a frog means turning a darker shade of green. And the Prince started to croak.

"*Ker-er-er … cakcakcak, cakcakcak; trrrriddle-iddle, gollup. Krakra-krak, urg, urg, gollup, gollup, gra-a-a-arr …*"

It was the saddest, soppiest love song in the

frog charts. And the Prince did it beautifully. All the girl frogs started to sigh. As for Gogglina, she just sat there, totally besotted.

"*Ka-raaaa … ka-raaaa … gollup, gollup … GLUMMMM!*" The Prince finished on a heart-breaking croak. For a moment there was silence. Then, all around the pond, girl frogs started to scream and pretend to faint.

Gogglina said, "*Wow …*"

The Prince asked in a small voice, "What do you think?"

Grandma Glugga stared at him. Then a single, big, fat tear rolled down her cheek and went *splot* into the pond.

"Well, croodle my nubkins," she said. "He *is* a frog!" She turned to Gogglina. "Go on, girl, what are you waiting for? Time wasted is time bewiggled! Kiss him!"

Gogglina went slowly towards the Prince. The Prince bent down. Gogglina looked up. The Prince puckered his mouth and shut his eyes.

Sssssss … MACK!

There was a greeny-yellow flash and a *bang*. When the smoke cleared, the Prince had vanished.

In his place was a drop-dead-gorgeous boy frog.

"*Wow!*" said Gogglina. She beamed at the Prince (we'd better call him Golp now) and gave a little wriggle.

Golp grinned at her. "Hey," he said, "that is *better*! Thanks, babe – I owe you one!"

He started to hop away. Gogglina's face fell. "Wait a minute!" she said, "Where are you going?"

"Uh?" Golp looked surprised. "Home, of course! To my girlfriend."

"Girlfriend?" Gogglina was horrified. "What about me?"

Golp laughed. "Look, you've done me a *big* favour, sure you have. But you're just a kid, right? My Glub's a *proper* girl!"

"Then why didn't *she* kiss you and turn you back?" wailed Gogglina.

"What? Kiss a *human?*" said Golp. "Get real, babe! Be seeing ya!"

And he leaped, *sproing*, away across the palace garden.

All the frogs looked at poor Gogglina. And

poor Gogglina stared sadly after Golp as he *sproinged* away, getting smaller with each jump. He disappeared. The frogs said nothing,

but crept away one by one, until only Gogglina and Grandma Glugga were left.

Gogglina started to cry. "He said I was beautiful …"

"What would he know?" snapped Grandma Glugga. "He's nothing but a low-down wamble-flinker. *Men!*"

"I'd never have kissed him if I'd known," said Gogglina miserably.

"Hmm," said Grandma. "That gives me an idea. Wait here!"

She jumped into the pond, and there was a lot of sploshing under the water. Then Grandma reappeared, wearing her best hat. She only wore her best hat when she meant to *do* something.

"Come on," she told Gogglina. "We're going visiting."

"Who are we going to visit?" Gogglina asked.

"A good friend of mine. She's a witch."

"A ... witch?" Gogglina gulped. "Is she ... wicked?"

"Oho, she is!" said Grandma. "Wily Wanda, the Well Wicked Witch, that's her! I got her crystal ball back for her once, when she dropped it in the river, so she owes me a favour."

"Wh-what do you want her to do?" asked Gogglina.

Grandma grinned widely. "I don't think Golp really likes being a frog. I think he'd much rather be a prince again. A pink, hairy, yukky, human prince! And *this* time –"

Gogglina started to grin, too. Poor Golp. No more lovely mud. No more delicious flies. Just cake and peanut butter and ice cream. And princesses. *Gruesome!*

"Yeah!" she said. "This time – no kissy, kissy!"

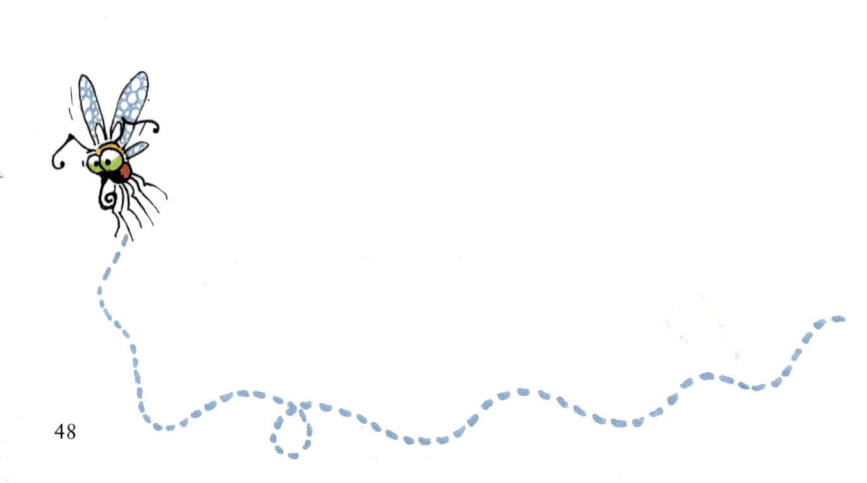